HOW THE WATER FEELS TO THE FISHES

Dave Eggers

M c SWEENEY'S BOOKS
SAN FRANCISCO

www.mcsweeneys.net

Copyright © 2007 Dave Eggers

Cover art by Jacob Magraw-Mickelson

ISBN-10: 1-932416-82-X
ISBN-13: 978-1-932416-82-4

CONTENTS

ONCE A YEAR

Once a year, she remembers that she is insignificant. Then she forgets again, because more than she is insignificant, she is forgetful.

ACCIDENT

You all get out of your cars. You are alone in yours, and there are three teenagers in theirs. The accident was your fault and you walk over to tell them this. Walking over to their car, an old and restored Camaro which you have ruined, it occurs to you that if the three teenagers are angry teenagers, this encounter could be very unpleasant. You pulled in to an intersection, obstructing them, and their car hit yours. They have every right to be upset, or livid, or even violent. As you approach, you see that their driver's side door won't open. The driver pushes against it, and you are reminded of scenes where drivers are stuck in sub-merged cars. Soon they all exit through the passenger side door and walk around the Camaro, inspecting the damage. "Just bought this today," the driver says. He is eighteen, blond, average in all ways. "Today?" you ask. You are a bad person, you think. You also think: What an odd car for a teenager to buy in the twenty-first century. "Yeah, today," he says, then sighs. You tell him that you are sorry. That you are so, so sorry. That it was your fault and that you will cover all costs. You exchange insurance information, and you find yourself, minute by minute, ever more thankful that none of these teenagers has punched you, or even made a remark about your being drunk, which you are not. You become more friendly with all of them, and you realize that you are much more connected to them, particularly to the driver, than would be possible in any other way. You have done him and his friends some psychic harm, and you jeopardized their health, and now you are so close you feel like you share a heart. He knows your name and you know his, and you almost killed him and because you got so close but didn't, you want to fall on him, weeping, because you are so lonely, so lonely always, and all contact is contact, and all contact makes us so grateful we want to cry and dance and cry and cry. In a moment of clarity you finally understand why boxers, who want so badly to hurt each other, can rest their heads on the shoulders of their opponent, can lean against one another like tired lovers, so thankful for a moment of rest.

OLD ENOUGH

He wanted to be old enough—old enough to hug anyone in any context. If he were old enough, he could meet someone and then throw his arms around him or her, laugh heartily, and move on, perhaps while mumbling to himself. No one would question it. They would say, "What a gregarious old fellow," and shake their heads, admiring. It would be nice to hug anyone, he thinks, and to comment liberally on the fitness of women and men, telling anyone he wished that their body was magnificent. He wanted to spread that kind of goodwill, and use creative adjectives while doing so. Splendid, spectacular, robust! *Your husband,* he would say, *has a splendid physique! Your wife, she is built so well—I love how she is shaped!* Wow, that would be good. Then he could kiss her. Kiss all the wives! He wants to kiss the wives, and use these words, and he wants to be able to whistle loudly in public. Already he whistles softly to himself, no tune in particular—just a rough blowing of air through his lips—but he wants to whistle tunes, and loudly, and he wants all who see and hear him to think, Well sure, he's of a different generation, the kindly sort who used to whistle happy songs to themselves. What a pleasure to see him! Those things he wants, the hugging and commenting and whistling, and he wants also to be able to forget things, to forget anything and everything, unintentionally and otherwise, without anyone assuming he is too callous to remember their names, their birthdays, their marital status, their trips to Old Havana and with whom. To be old enough! He could do all these things if he were old enough. If he were old enough, he could stay home. He could stay out late. He could draw conclusions and burn bridges. He could own a gun, many guns, and store shelves of canned goods in his basement. He could care about some things and not care about most things. At parties, he could wander away from boring conversations—he wouldn't have to say a word, he would just blink absentmindedly and float away. Yes! He could kick dogs, even if softly, then roll around with them and become lifelong friends. He could eat bell peppers, eat them constantly. He wants to be able to walk through the woods and down the hill and to the beach and forget how to get home (or pretend to have forgotten). Some kindly family would drive him home and he could tell them untrue stories of his time in Algeria, how he helped make that one movie, how he held the boom and even worked as a special advisor to the dynamite crew. They would drop him at his home and think, What a fascinating old fellow! Once home, he could take off all his clothes, put on a turban, and then sit down at a rolltop desk—he would own a rolltop desk if he were old enough—and he could go through his mail, throwing out all envelopes not postmarked on Tuesday. He could return invitations with a boldly written "NO, please NO," and everyone would find it charming. He could send letters to the editors of major newspapers complaining about an undefinable pain in his side. He could sleep through weddings and avoid all funerals. He could narrow his aperture. Or open it up, and keep it open, always. He could be everywhere at all times. He could burn himself alive, he could spread his own ashes over the people he might have hugged while laughing. That kind of thing they would never forget. Or he could study whales, become better with the whales than almost anyone. At the whale conventions, he could talk to the young researchers with their young bodies and tell them all about the whales and their bodies, how magnificent they all are.

SHE NEEDS A NEW JOURNAL

The one she has is problematic. To get to the present, she needs to page through the past, and when she does, she remembers things, and her new journal entries become, for the most part, reactions to the days she regrets, wants to correct, rewrite.

SOONER

The man is fifty-two years old, and he is dating a woman of twenty-seven. His name is Gunther and his face looks like that of Sammy Davis Jr., if SDJ were white and less handsome. Gunther is not German or Austrian, but Canadian, of French descent, and does not know why he was named Gunther. After two unsuccessful marriages and three fortunes made and lost, he has recently met a woman, a hedge-fund trader named Kim, who likes him a great deal for what appear to be the right reasons—because he is charming, because he is still attractive in his way, because he is mature and steady and yet still willing to try new things, like windsurfing, which he took up after seeing the John Kerry photo. After three dates, each more lengthy and affectionate, all is well between the two of them, and Gunther is so happy that he must make sure, when holding Kim—for thus far they have done no more than kiss and hug—not to groan. Her skin is so dewy, her shape so taut, that he has difficulty, when they embrace, holding back a sigh so loud and thankful that she would certainly be unnerved if she heard it. But really, how does he find himself in a position like this, to be holding this young person, who is smarter than he, who is witty and warm and can dance like they do in music videos? His sigh, which he allows at home, alone, in bed and in the shower, is grateful for this chance, but this sigh also says I am scared she will leave. It says Maybe this is all some terrible hoax or misunderstanding. It says Soon she will see me naked and flee. And it is these fears that cause him to sigh alone, and to suppress his sighs while holding her supple waist. This will be temporary, he knows. His hold on this youthful beauty, this person within which the blood moves quicker and the synapses fire faster and whose hands are soft in his—he thinks of a dragon's grip on a newborn—this person will slip away soon enough, and this and all things transient are what cause his groans. Groans he must suppress lest they cause her to leave sooner.

THE COMMERCIALS OF NORWAY

She is in Oslo on business. She is in a bar, after her meetings, sipping a cocktail she cannot pronounce; it is her fourth and she is feeling sublime. On the TV above her she has seen three commercials in a row that she has found witty. The commercials have been in Norwegian, but still she has seen the humor in them. The humor is gestural and subtle and does not rely on knowing the language. She laughed out loud at the last one, when the flamingo broke that lamp. *Huh,* the woman thinks. *Not bad.* She wishes people in her own country could see these commercials; she is sure they would love them. She wonders how the commercials might appear on television in her country—maybe on some kind of special show. Would any network run a special, a half-hour presentation of the commercials of Norway? Probably not, she thinks, ordering another drink. The people of her country probably don't need more commercials. There are a lot of commercials on TV where she comes from, and, come to think of it, the commercials in her own country are pretty funny too. On the whole, they're probably better than the commercials of Norway. These three witty ones tonight were most likely the best of the bunch, she thinks, while drinking more drink. The rest are shit, probably, she thinks. The commercials of Norway are shit. Yes, she thinks. They fucking suck. Fuck them, she thinks. Fuck the commercials of Norway, she says out loud, and sips on her drink, which also sucks.

LILY

Tell me your secrets, she tells her friends. Tell me anything, she says, because I will forget it all. And the friends laugh. They know she is serious. She is a good friend because she will listen, and ask questions, and commiserate, and she will tell no one their secrets, because she will forget their secrets almost instantly. Because though she does care about her friends, she does not care about their secrets.

THE BOY THEY DIDN'T
TAKE PICTURES OF

The boy, Charles, was part of a family of seven—four children, two parents, a grandmother they called Pippy. He was not the oldest and not the youngest but was eleven when he noticed something: everywhere in the house were pictures of all of the members of the family, together and alone, but nowhere was there a picture of Charles. He said nothing about it, because he made himself believe that it was not true, that somewhere—some upstairs bathroom or basement hallway—he would be proven wrong, he would find a picture of himself. Did he ever investigate this closely? Never, of course. When he was fourteen, he spent a good deal of time at the house of a friend named Alex. Alex's mother, named Scarlet and looking that way, liked to take pictures of Alex's friends; she had a wall where she displayed them all. But as the months went by, and Charles's time at Alex's house implied that he should be on the wall too, nothing of the kind happened. Scarlet smiled at him, spoke to him kindly, but never asked him to sit on the fence in the front yard, where all the other boys posed. Again Charles said nothing, because he figured it was an oversight only, one that, if pointed out, would make him seem gauche or needy or strange. Many years later, now in his twenties, Charles dated a woman, Reah, who kept pictures on her shelves. Small gold and seashelled frames held photos of her friends and sisters and even her ex-boyfriends—who were now her good friends and (how nice!) called often. But after nine months together, there were no pictures of Charles on the shelves. Reah had never even taken his photo, or asked a stranger to take their picture together. Again, Charles said nothing. But with each successive slight, from childhood till the present, with each odd instance of his seemingly lifelong invisibility, he wondered: Was he ugly? He wasn't, he knew this, but nor was he handsome. Aha! He did have an unshapely nose, and an incongruous chin, and some scars from acne that potholed his cheeks. But was that it? Did the people he knew simply prefer the more photogenic of their friends and family? He knew this was too simple, too crude, too enraging and wretched to be doubted for a moment.

THE FIGHTS NOT FOUGHT

She could not remember where she ate dinner the night before, or whom she had met last week in that walnut-paneled room. She could not recall the names of the streets where she once lived, or the date of her own father's birthday. But she could remember the fights she did not fight. There were so many, and they haunted her with a stabbing, shaming pain. People had told her to choose her battles, and she had chosen some and neglected others, and now the neglected came to her like an army of lost children. She should have chosen them all, she thought to herself, as she buried another friend. She should have chosen every one.

THE HORROR

Sandra never read horror novels, because everything scared her. Or rather, when she was young, just about everything scared her, so she never watched thrillers or slasher movies, much less read anything by King or Straub or Lovecraft. Her imagination was easily ignited, and the line between fiction and reality, for her, was much too malleable. Often, after a vivid dream, it took her days to come to terms with the fact that the dream was indeed a dream, and not something more—an alternate reality, a prophecy, a message from dead persons known or unknown. Nevertheless, when she was thirty years old, she had an idea for a horror novel or movie or perhaps both. The entire thing, she decided, would take place during the day. The only other scary movie she could think of that also took place during daylight hours was *Jaws,* and that didn't count, because the world underwater, as we all know, is much like night. Her movie would be light the entire time, and, even better, the night would be the time when everyone—all those oppressed by the terror—would rest. Everyone would get a good night's sleep each night. Having settled all that, Sandra was very satisfied. As a reward for having such a good brain, she walked to her fridge and made herself a sandwich with two types of bread, and speared it with a toothpick. All she needed now was to decide what exactly would be scary, and how people would die or be torn apart or maimed. She stood, eating her sandwich, and then had another revelation: What if no one died? Couldn't that be scary, in its own way? It certainly would be unexpected. Now, she felt, she was onto something. A horror movie that took place during the day and in which no one was killed. But what would it be about? What would happen? The movie, she figured, could feature many surprises—people jumping out from closets and jabbing things quickly. That could be made suspenseful throughout, with the audience not knowing exactly when, for example, the jumping-out and jabbing-at would happen. But then again, wouldn't it be kind of scary—and better all around—if you (a) didn't know when or where jumping-out would occur, and also (b) didn't know whether or not such things would occur at all? Imagine watching the movie, fully expecting that something would happen, only to sit waiting, throughout, thus becoming ever more tense? She had now put down her sandwich, because her head was working too quickly and brilliantly; she dared not distract it with chewing. So an all-daylight horror movie with only the pretense of suspense, only the promise (to be broken) of chases, of danger and violence and untimely death. She would have her characters wander throughout, talking tensely—or laconically!—eyeing each other and every doorway warily. Or perhaps with great nonchalance. What if, she thought, her characters walked calmly through their lives, without threats, without suspense or shadows, expecting nothing and receiving nothing? Now, she thought, that is horror.

HOW THE WATER FEELS TO THE FISHES

Like the fur of a chinchilla. Like the cleanest tooth. Yes, the fishes say, this is what it feels like. People always ask the fishes, "What does the water feel like to you?" and the fishes are always happy to oblige. Like feathers are to other feathers, they say. Like powder touching ash. When the fishes tell us these things, we begin to understand. We begin to think we know what the water feels like to the fishes. But it's not always like fur and ash and the cleanest tooth. At night, they say, the water can be different. At night, when it's very cold, it can be like the tongue of a cat. At night, when it's very very cold, the water is like cracked glass. Or honey. Or forgiveness, they say, ha ha. When the fishes answer these questions—which they are happy to do— they also ask why. They are curious, fish are, and thus they ask, Why? Why do you want to know what the water feels like to the fishes? And we are never quite sure. The fishes press further. Do you breathe air? they ask. The answer, we say, is yes. Well then, they say, What does the air feel like to you? And we do not know. We think of air and we think of wind, but that's another thing. Wind is air in action, air on the move, and the fishes know this. Well then, they ask again, what does the air feel like? And we have to think about this. Air feels like air, we say, and the fishes laugh mirthlessly. Think! they say. Think, they say, now gentler. And we think and we guess that it feels like hair, thousands of hairs, swaying ever so slightly in breezes microscopic. The fishes laugh again. Do better, think harder, they say. It feels like language, we say, and they are impressed. Keep going, they say. It feels like blood, we say, and they say, No, no, that's not it. The air is like being wanted, we say, and they nod approvingly. The air is like getting older, they say, and they touch our arms gently.

HOW TO DO IT

The woman, named Puma, was forty-four, shaped like a gymnast, and had too many friends. She had lived in the same city, full of Mormons, for twenty-five years, and she was not impetuous or jealous or callous or cruel. Thus, the friends she had made twenty-five years ago were still her friends now, and because her job—she was a veterinary surgeon, specializing in toucans—brought her in contact with new people all the time, she added friends with now-troubling regularity. Which was fine, it was nice to have new companions, but at this point Puma could no longer be a good friend to all of them—to even half of them. She did the calculations one day: ten friends from her first few years in the city, and (at the very least) three more added every year thereafter. This brought her to a total, now, of about eighty-five good friends and close acquaintances, and this number, given birthdays and anniversaries and sympathy calls and favors and lunches and various gift-giving showers, made her life untenable. Every day was something, every day was everyone. She couldn't enjoy her time with any one of them, knowing that she was neglecting the rest. And she certainly couldn't enjoy time alone, because at this point even an hour to herself—when she hadn't, for example, seen William and Jeanette's new baby, now five months old!—was decadent, selfish, and utterly foreign. Her friends had made her unfriendly, her chums had sapped her charm. Something had to be done; she had to make a break. So she stopped answering her phone, and no longer took walks. She ordered her groceries online, and pretended her email didn't work. And for a day, one glorious day, this worked. But they found her. Of course they did. They found her at work, at her home. They dropped cute notes in her mailbox, fastened them under her car's windshield wipers. They did so because her friends were good friends, were persistent and not to be easily put off. They worried, they wished her well. But this only made Puma more perturbed, more desperate to be free, and more determined to bring them all together, for a grand dinner one night, where she would deal with the problem once and for all. It was extreme, yes, but also necessary, and thankfully possible, for among her too many friends (and the only ones she would spare) she had a caterer, an expert in untraceable and fast-acting poisons, and an excellent attorney.

GO-GETTERS

The woman is a young woman. She wants to make a living as a photographer, but at the moment she is temping at a company that publishes books about wetlands preservation. On her days off she takes pictures, and today she is sitting in her car, across the street from a small grocery store called "The Go-Getters Market." The store is located in a very poor neighborhood of her city—the store's windows are barred and at night a roll-down steel door covers the facade. The woman thus finds the name "Go-Getters" an interesting one, because it is clear that the customers of the market are anything but go-getters. They are drunkards and prostitutes and transients, and the young photographer thinks that if she can get the right picture of some of these people entering the store, she will make a picture that would be considered trenchant, or even poignant—either way, the product of a sharp and observant eye. So she sits in her Toyota Camry, which her parents gave her because it was two years old and they wanted something new, and she waits for the right poor person to enter or leave the store. She has her window closed, but will open it when the right person appears, and then will shoot that person under the sign that says "Go-Getters." This, for the viewer of her photograph when it is displayed—first in a gallery, then in the hallway of a collector's second home, and later in a museum when she has her retrospective—will prove that she, the photographer, has an exceptional eye for irony and hypocrisy, for the inequities and injustices of life, its absurdity perfect and absolute.

DEEPER

Under the sky is the earth, and under the earth is the water. Under the water is the rock, and under the rock there is fire. Under the fire are the bones of the mammals who could not cope. Next to them are the girls who thought he had a nice smile so why not. Just under them are the boys who thought they could swim all the way across. Next to them are the men of God who took and took and took. Under them is more water, more fire, more stone. Next to the stone and the fire are the heroes who would not listen. Below them are the heroes who listened too much. Then there is a layer of oil and diamonds and silver, and a series of pockets where they keep the women who shook their babies and told no one and then ran. Below those pockets there is the lava and under the lava is the sandstone and all the people who thought life would be long enough to do evil for just a while, that there would be time to say sorry later.

THE BATTLE BETWEEN

It was a great battle. You probably heard about it already, so why go on about it here? It was really good, just the best—very intense, hard-fought, and then sort of unclear, at the end, who won. Afterward, there were parades held by both sides, and, ten years later, some movies were made about the whole thing, and these were watched by the citizenry with a sense of grave responsibility. The end. Now we will spend this next half page together, talking about the only thing appropriate at the beginning of June, and that is the outdoor shower, and the advantages thereof. The outdoor shower is: the only way to make a broken woman whole. It can: lighten the load of a burdened man. It will: calm a restless mind. It will: create milk from bile, and cotton from cancer. The outdoor shower must: be experienced to be believed. It will not: disappoint. It will not: come to you. You must: go to it. Yes, leave your seat. Yes, walk through the door. Yes, find a sky that's blue and a sun that's warm, or a sky that's white and a sun that's hot. Find some grass or trees or ivy. Find yourself alone. Find a shower-head, or a hose, or a bucket with holes punched beneath. Bring some water. The water cannot be too cold or too hot; the water must be wet but never ostentatious. Now take off your clothes. Do not wear sandals, do not wear clogs. Put your clothes where they can't be seen, and begin the water. Look up as the water comes to you, laughing—not at you, with you—while it falls downward, celebrated by the sun on its descent. Each drop is given light; this is only fair. Now push the water around your body. Touch your wet skin and feel somewhat sexual. Now strangely pure. Now sexual again. Now like an animal. Now like an elf, thin and immortal and fearless in battle. Now take some water in your mouth. Return it to the land. Look up again at the water, still coming to you, all of the droplets giggling like babies. Let them fall. Now you understand. Let them fall. Now you know why water falls, why children fall, why everything falls. Water falls so we can stand under, await-ing and undestroyed.

THERE ARE DIFFERENT KINDS

She is thinking about pain. In one day, she has suffered two kinds: at noon, she received news of a horrific sort of betrayal, and at four-thirty, she dropped a barbell on her foot. Now she is lying on her couch, with ice on her foot and with demons running amok in her head, spinning around, their tails poking her, their laughs wild, jagged with scorn. She is waiting, on her couch, trying not to get too excited. She has always thought of herself as rational about pain. She knows that its duration is intrinsically limited, that it must end at some point, so with physical pain she has always been stoic and rational—to the point that she has seemed, to those who know her, robotic, almost insensate. She has broken her limbs and sliced her fingers and has barely winced. She suffered a slipped disk and pushed twins through her birth canal and in neither case did she weep or cry out. This is because she has reminded herself that every minute will bring a measurable diminution of the pain, so she sees no point in participating too much in the high-low theatricality of it all. She would be concerned only if the pain did not decrease on a more or less steadily downward path—but it has never diverged from this steadily downward path. However. However, the mental pain is different. She has never remembered, with any clarity, the pain she suffered between her legs or in her limbs—the memory of physical pain is so fleeting; thus women who bear multiple children—but the pain of lies, the pain of insults, of treachery, abandonments, these pains can come back to her, years or decades later, with incredible clarity. And they do, they do, they do! They lunge at her, with no shame about being so old; they have a permanent and exaggerrated sense of their own importance. And she is now lying on the couch, dispassionately nursing her foot, while her mind is flooding, panicking about this new betrayal, which came to her today, on a postcard. It was so small! How could something so small... A beautiful picture of Bucharest on one side, and just the most violent scrawlings on the other—the most reckless and slashing words! Only twenty-two words but they slash at her and she knows that they will never leave her. Will they? God, this pain! She tries to map it, calculate its half-life: How long will these twenty-two words have power? How much will she need to drink, and for how many days or weeks, to sleep each night? She will watch so much TV, see so many movies with her friends and acquaintances and ex-boyfriends and alone; she will ask every friend she has to join her for every lunch and dinner and cocktails; she will sleep with four new men, three of them friends, one of them her doorman. And still the demons will flick their tails and laugh their laughs, repeating the twenty-two words, especially those last six, all the while hissing their consonants with great relish. And the end? Will there be an end to it? She knows that this particular betrayal might be with her for many years, and she grasps for ways to expel it, the very fact of it, before it gains too great a foothold within her. She would do anything, give anything, to have the pains reversed: she would happily live for years, on and off, with the pain of her swelling foot, of any wound really—she would push babies through her legs, one each week!—if she could only know that in a few hours this pain could be counted on to recede, to behave.

ALBERTO

Alberto Gonzales and his father broke the upper crust with each step. Below the crust the snow was dry and granular, a feel of both cotton and sand. Alberto and his father were walking home from the grandmother's house, where they had turned her over and washed her.

Alberto's family was now in a new house. Two months before, they had moved from their grandmother's house, where they had lived the nine years of Alberto's life, to this new house, about three miles away.

The air was heavy with cold, and breathing it in felt to Alberto like inhaling glass and expelling wool. Sixteen inches of snow had fallen in two days and nothing had been plowed. The car Alberto's father drove would not make it through this, so they had walked. Their grandmother was alone but for the neighbor girl, Kelly, who was dependable but sometimes needed relief. They were walking up a hill in the park, a short-cut that would take them under the highway and to a field that led through the unincorporated area and to their house.

"I figured out how to scare your mom," Alberto's father said.

It was the first thing Alberto or his father had said during the walk.

"How do you mean?" Alberto said.

"You know that window next to her desk?"

Alberto did. His mother's office was on the second floor. He nodded.

"Well, she's not used to anything happening right out her window, right? It's on the second floor, eighteen feet above the ground."

Alberto nodded again. His mother's window, over her desk where she did bookkeeping and tax returns, overlooked the backyard, and beyond it, the unincorporated land.

"Well, I've been thinking that a great way to really scare her would be to jump out right there and yell like crazy. She'd scream like a banshee."

Alberto didn't know what a banshee was, but his father had said this before, so he assumed a banshee was either someone who screamed a lot, or screamed loudly and well. Alberto pictured his mother screaming.

"I would just get up on the ladder and pop out, and yell Wah!" his father said.

They were walking under the highway now and his

father's voice was louder, and his Wah! stayed in the underpass for some time.

As they were passing through the dim corridor Alberto wondered how loudly his mother would scream, and how long afterward it would take her to calm down. He wondered if his mother would find the scaring funny, or if she would be angry.

Alberto wanted to scare his mother.

"I want to scare her," he said.

"You can watch me do it," his father said. They were now in the light again. "Actually, maybe it's not such a great idea. Your mom doesn't like being scared."

Alberto took in a quick breath.

"She does!" Alberto said.

"No, I don't think she does. That one time I did it she was mad for a pretty long while."

Alberto had heard about that. After seeing a suspenseful movie on TV, his father had hidden in the backseat of the car. He knew Alberto's mom would go to the convenience store, which she did every night to get fresh bagels for the next morning, so he had snuck out to the car and hidden in the backseat. He had stayed there, in the backseat, while she started out on the highway and then exited onto the frontage road. He waited until the third stoplight, when the road was dark and quiet. Then he jumped up and yelled "Wah!"

They had stayed there, at the intersection, for an hour.

"I got an earful," his father said.

"She'll like it this time," Alberto said.

"No, I don't think so. It was a bad idea."

Alberto was furious. The scaring was something that was about to happen, the event looming ahead like a holiday, and now it would not happen. He felt dizzy. He would have to argue with his father to ensure any possibility of it happening, and even then it probably would not happen.

As they walked, the snow breaking underfoot, Alberto explored other ways he could jump in front of his mother's window. He could do it himself, but the ladder was too heavy for him to lift and raise. He could jump from the tree nearby, but that was too far. He could somehow swing down from the rooftop on a rope, the rope perhaps tied to the chimney. He wondered if they had any rope that would be strong enough.

As they came across the cornfield and saw the house in the distance, Alberto pleaded with his father to scare his mother. His father told him to drop it. Alberto begged. His father stopped responding.

When they pushed through the hedge at the perimeter of their yard, the branches throwing snow at them, they could see Alberto's mother in her second-floor window, her soft oval face painted in ochre.

Alberto's father went inside, stomping his feet on the porch, releasing the snow. Alberto went to the garage and found the dead frog he'd been keeping in a jar. He dropped it onto his father's worktable and cut its limbs off, one by one, then its belly, stem to stern.

YOU STILL KNOW THAT BOY

He was very angry at fourteen, fifteen, in summer and winter, at home or in the world. So angry that his face contorted in photos. The camera was a question and his face did not know the answer.

NO SAFE HARBOR

There are three people in a living room in Montreal. There is a young couple, Thom and Justine, and there is Justine's great uncle Grant. Six months ago Thom and Justine lost their seven-year-old daughter when she fell from the roof of a friend's home. Thom and Justine worked together, doing consulting at home, before the accident, but now they don't work much. They watch TV and rent movies, and they've repainted much of their house. Thom drinks aquavit and orange juice at night, to help bring sleep, and Justine naps during the day. In Florida, two months ago, Grant's wife, Hattie, died, and he has come out to Montreal to see friends he has not seen in years, and to see Thom and Justine. He called them two hours prior to his arrival and they greeted him at the door. But now they are all in the living room, and no one is talking. Grant, looking at his hands, comments on the new-paint smell in the house. Justine and Thom apologize and suggest they sit outside. Grant insists they stay where they are, that the smell is fine. So they stay and sit, and they don't eat or drink, and no one says much. For ten minutes, they watch the cat try to remove its claws from the Persian rug. Within an hour, with a sigh, Grant leaves, shuffling to his rental car and then away. Years later, when Grant has passed on too, Thom and Justine will remember that day, when Grant came to visit, the last time they saw him. He came looking for comfort, Justine will say. I think so, Thom will say. But we didn't even offer him a glass of water, Justine will say. We were useless, Thom will say. To be honest, Thom will say, I just couldn't muster any feelings about Hattie's death. I figured she'd lived long enough. Grant wanted to commiserate, and I didn't find the two deaths even remotely comparable. Yeah, I wanted him gone, Justine will say, nodding, remembering. Gone-gone, Thom will say. Me too, Justine will say. Yes. Me too. I wanted all those types of people gone.

THE BOUNTY

In her kitchen, she saw many things she would like to eat. On the counter, there was a bunch of new bananas, yellow as a Van Gogh chair, and two apples, pristine. The cabinet was open and she saw a box of crackers, a new box of cereal, a tube of curved chips. She felt overwhelmed, seeing all of the food there, that it was all hers. And there was more in the refrigerator! There were juices, half a melon, a dozen bagels, salmon, a steak, yogurt in a dozen colors. It would take her a week to eat all of this food. She does not deserve this, she thought. It really isn't fair, she thought. You're correct, God said, and then struck dead 65,000 Malaysians.

ON MAKING HIM A GOOD MAN BY CALLING HIM A GOOD MAN

Stuart has the face of a Scottish warrior. He has been told this, though he is unsure if this means that he has a historically accurate and fierce Highlands look, or that he simply looks like a particular actor from *Braveheart*. Stuart has been friends with Margaret since they were very small. Margaret, soft in every way, recently married Phillipe, who is an idiot. Stuart feels no jealously toward Phillipe, for he and Margaret were never romantic, and he actually wanted to like Phillipe, from the start he tried to like Phillipe, but Phillipe has always made this difficult because Phillipe is a moron. Phillipe does not work, or does not work often, and feels no guilt at all about allowing Margaret to pay for food, for car repairs that he makes necessary, and for rent. When he has his own money, he goes on sportfishing vacations without Margaret. As we said, he is an idiot. Is he charming? He is not. Is he handsome? Passably. What, then, is his appeal? The narrator is not sure. Anyway, one day, Stuart and Phillipe were standing near each other at one of the many birthdays, bar mitzvahs, and christenings at which they find themselves. As they were talking about sportfishing, which at least means Phillipe will not talk about the ineffectivness of the U.N., Phillipe noticed, at the corner of the building, a young boy being taunted by three others. Before Stuart could react, Phillipe sprinted toward the scrum, and chased away the offenders, and was soon consoling the young boy, who after a few minutes was laughing at Phillipe's jokes. When Phillipe returned to the gathering, Stuart, who saw the entire scene unfold, patted Phillipe on the back and said, "Phillipe, you're a good man." Stuart said this very seriously, because he was greatly impressed by Philippe's heroics, and because the words *good man* are used with the utmost sincerity in his family. In fact, the primary aspiration of the men in his family is to be called, by their father or grandfather or great uncle Daniel, a "good man." So Stuart called Phillipe a good man, and though he felt initially that he might have jumped the gun, that one decent act doesn't necessarily define a man, Stuart was surprised to see that over the next weeks and months, Phillipe seemed to change. He stood straighter, he showed up on time. He was kind to, even chivalrous to, Margaret, and undertook a steady job. He sent her and two of her friends to a weekend spa, and fixed the broken door to her closet. Phillipe never said a word about being called a good man, and Stuart couldn't be sure that the words had any effect on him. But the change in him was clear: he was becoming what Stuart had called him, a good man. Stuart wondered if we, all or any of us, are so easily improved. If all we need is this kind of semantic certainty. If to be named is to be realized. If once something like that is settled—I *am* a good man—we no longer need to struggle, to guess, to err.

THOUGHTFUL THAT WAY

The people who do your dreams are like the people in your life who give very thoughtful gifts. The people who organize your nighttime dreams are paying close attention to the things you see and hear during the day. You notice a certain yellow car and they note your noticing and they file this information away. In a magazine you see mention of a junior-high friend and you quickly forget it. But the people who do your dreams have taken note of this friend-sighting, and in three months they will place this friend in your dream about your stepfather killing your uncle with two hand-saws and a pair of pliers. Your junior-high friend will be watching from the bleachers, because the people who organize your dreams are thoughtful that way.

WE CAN WORK IT OUT

I'm not the one to ask about this. Lately everyone's been saying, Hey, man, what's the deal? Why do all the bears of North America dislike E. M. Forster? And everyone expects me to have all the answers, just because I hang out with some bears sometimes. It's messed up, right? The truth is, I don't know much. I really don't. Okay, listen, this is what I know: a while ago, some bears and I were gathered at Yosemite, which is where bears sometimes gather. It's loose, it's cool, it's whatever. They were all there, all the important ones, some black bears and brown bears and a few grizzlies, and they started talking about Henry James, and for some reason that led into E. M. Forster, and, yeah, these bears just started going off. It was ugly. I honestly haven't seen them like that since someone brought up Austen. Yeah. If you think these bears hate Forster, you should hear them on the subject of *Emma*. Man, they hate *Emma*. Again, don't ask me to explain it. I don't get it. Just don't talk to them about *Emma,* or Forster, or early Dickens. God, early Dickens makes them insane. Talk about Dickens, and they start eating bark, and sometimes tires. It's messed up. But if you're looking for answers, don't come to me. I can't keep up with all the questions from you people. I want to help, but I don't know how. Believe me, I wish they were more mellow about all this. I can say this: the brown bears are less dead-set against Austen, and the grizzlies really only have a problem with *The Pickwick Papers*. I don't know if that helps at all, but there it is. In the meantime, I'll keep track of where they stand on everything, and I'll make inroads where I can.

NO ONE KNOWS

For years it had been assumed. One day there were record players—phonographs, they were called then—and they conjured music with a needle touching a flat piece of rotating vinyl. It seemed improbable by all who saw it, but no one questioned it; there were wars to fight and babies to scar. Every so often someone said, Excuse me, who invented this thing, anyway, and how in tarnation does it work? But then this person would be either ignored or mocked or both; once such a person was feathered (but not tarred). And so it happened that decade after decade passed, and no one questioned this device that no one actually knew anything about, and which made no sense to anyone whatsoever. This went on for so long, too long, but finally there was a man, his name was Donald, and in 1986 he wondered aloud how it could be that a needle touching a piece of vinyl could bring forth music. He looked far and wide, and there were no answers. For a hundred years everyone assumed there was someone who knew, and now the truth came out: no one knew. But now Donald had asked and people felt allowed to wonder, quietly and aloud too. Quickly it became a question posited all over the newspapers and talk shows of the world, and in books, and scientists gave up trying to discern the source and reasoning behind the pyramids of Egypt, and instead wondered about the record players, why and how and who. Finally, after ten years of questions and intense research, one of the scientists, also named Donald (no relation), decided to open up a record player and look inside. He did so in a lead tank, of course, and while wearing bulletproof gear and thick boots. When he finally got the top open, he found a group of very small people, tiny people, really, inside, and around them a mess of instruments, sheet music, and microphones. They looked up at Donald, not so much startled as annoyed, and Donald apologized. He closed up the record player, the mystery solved. I have found the answer, he told the world that night, it works just like the radio.

THE ISLAND FROM THE WINDOW

From your window you see an island. Every day you see this island. During the day it is bright, sailboats circling like toys, but at night it is unlit, uninhabited, darker than black. The daytime island is the one you know, but the island at night is the one you remember. All those faces so close as you lay, those many hands. You know what happened on that island, and have often thought you should move away from your home, from this view. There was a hammer, there was a fire. There were screams of laughter then a brief wail when it was no longer funny. A missing candle, a flashlight emptied of its power, a pile of shoes, a belt, the silence all through dawn. There was running, there was a hole you had to dig with your hands. It was so long ago, was it not? Was it yesterday? You should leave. Your mother, the only other one who knows what happened, has said you should leave. But you do not leave and you will not leave. You will stay close, you will look out at the black shape of the island every night not because of what happened there but because of what has not happened since. Nothing has happened since. Nothing at all.

THE ANGER OF THE HORSES

Last week we let all the horses go. It seemed the right thing to do. We tore down the fences, burned the bridles and the saddles, and told the horses they were free. At first they hesitated. "Go, go," we said. "Go." And so they went, up over the hill, across the plain and into the mountains. Two days later they returned. "We're bored," they said. So we sat with the horses for a while, trying to think of something for them to do. Before we could think of anything, the horses had an idea of their own. "Let's kill all the rabbits!" they said, their black eyes alight. "Let's kill all those goddamned rabbits!" they added. The horses became more and more inflamed as they talked about the details of the plan. "We'll run and find them, help flush them out," they said, "and then you can shoot them since you have the guns." They were pacing and snorting, shaking their manes and tails, ready to get started. It turns out the horses had hated the rabbits for a long, long time.

CALIFORNIA MOVED WEST

It was strange when it happened. The fault line shook and opened up and the state fell away. It broke off and drifted into the Pacific, late one summer day. It really happened, people thought. All those years, all those jokes, and here it goes and actually happens. People waited to see what would happen next, but they were disappointed. Exhilarating as that first day was, California was thereafter just there in the ocean, two or so miles away, with everything else pretty much the same—the lettuce farms, the skiing. They built a few new bridges, and the airlines added some flights.

HOW THE AIR FEELS TO THE BIRDS

They act as if they had never heard the question before. The what? they say. The air? What about it? We smile and rephrase the question: What does the air feel like to you, you being a bird, able to fly and all? Finally they seem to understand, and they meditate on this awhile. And then they begin: The air to us is a brother, a sister. We are intrigued, and lean in closer. The air, they continue, now quieter. We lean in yet farther. They peck us in the eye and laugh wickedly. Birds are bastards, every one of them.

THE MAN WHO

The man who invented hanging, who first proposed that a person could be killed quickly and theatrically with a noose and a trapdoor, cannot remember his motivation for having invented this. Now he is dead and wanders through a scarlet nether region, but he cannot escape the opprobrium of his peers, suspect as they are, for what he has done. He lives, in a manner of speaking, among so many others who have misbehaved in one life or another and are thus condemned, and yet he is singled out for particular abuse. Every day someone new to the lower realms and still angry about being there will approach him, finger wagging. You're the one! they always yell. How could you? And the thing of it is, he really doesn't know. This was a thousand years ago and he was a young man, only twenty, with the sleepy eyes of his mother. He wasn't a sadist. He didn't torture animals, he didn't dream of ways to kill mammals and men. But he did create the first noose, the first gallows; that much is true, and though he could not remember why he did it, he could not deny doing it. He attempts, though, to defend himself, to place his discovery in context. People have thought of everything—will think of everything! he says. Some person, probably not unlike myself, centuries ago thought to eat the least appetizing-looking animals—mussels, squid, crickets, boars. And why? Because there was opportunity. Because there was hunger. Because there was boredom. Some person, not unlike myself, thought to build homes on the steepest of hillsides, on tidelands, on fault lines, and in deserts. And why? Because there was opportunity. Because there was hunger and boredom. Some person, not unlike myself, he says, thought to build homes on the steepest of hillsides, on tidelands, on fault lines, in deserts. And why? Because there was need. Because there was greed and boredom. Some person, not unlike myself, he says, thought to test fragrances on rabbits, thought to inject cancer into mice and monkeys. Someone, not unlike myself, he says, now thinking he's on to something, thought of drawing and quartering, of tarring and feathering, of waterboarding and the iron maiden. And why? Because the brain, like water, seeks a downward path. Everything will be tried, he says. Every kind of person will kill every other kind of person in every kind of way, says the man who invented the noose and cannot remember why. Simply because they can, and there is time.

OLDER THAN

When you have a sibling and that sibling is older than you, often, when you are a boy and wanting to break the world and put it in your pocket, you want to be older than this sibling. Someday you will be older, you think.

But you cannot be older, your sibling says. Never will you be older. The older will always be older. You do not want to accept this, but you must. It is the rightness of the world.

But what if it happens that one day you are older? What if it happens that one day your sibling's heart stops, and they no longer get older, while you continue to age?

Then you will be older.

STEVE AGAIN

There was a dog named Steve and he had been running for years. Every day when the sun rose he ran toward it, and when he tired, he slept, only to run again when he woke. He ran through dry hills and wet marshes, over shallow rivers and fields that spread wide and balance-beam straight.

Steve had told some stories when he was younger, but now, he realized, it had been so long since he'd used his voice, his real voice. He had seen so few souls along his journey; there was almost no one who would listen. So he had been quiet, almost completely quiet for so long, save for the howling and breathing and barking he did out of habit.

But one day as he ran along the cliffside—which may or may not be the end of the world—he thought, with a dizzying rush to the head, he was ready to tell another story. He had seen so much over these years that he thought, Okay, maybe it's time. Maybe it's time to say what happened. Isn't that what the poet says, Just say what happened?

So then he turned back, running faster than before, looking for the right people to tell.

Acknowledgments

Thanks to the staff of McSweeney's for helping cobble this little collection of mine together, and to Sarah and Deb for allowing this scruffy book to rub shoulders with their more refined work. Thanks be to the editors at the *Guardian* in London, who first accepted the idea of these short-shorts, and who first published a handful of the stories found between these covers. Thanks also to the people of Penguin UK, for first binding some of these stories together in their Penguin 30s series, which was well-colored and also came in a (larger) box. Finally, I'd like to extend my thanks to Lydia Davis, whose work reminded me of the many forms a story might take, and what a piece of prose is and is not obligated to do, and at what length. Fans of hers will undoubtedly see a few pieces herein that might generously be called homages (and might be called far worse). For those readers who have not read Lydia Davis, you are urged to do so. She is terrifyingly good.